Ellie Ultra is published by Stone Arch Books,
A Capstone Imprint
1710 Roe Crest Drive
North Mankato, Minnesota 56003
www.mycapstone.com

Library of Congress Cataloging-in-Publication Data is
available on the Library of Congress website.

ISBN: 978-1-4965-3143-8 (hardcover) — 978-1-4965-3147-6
(paperback) — 978-1-4965-3151-3 (ebook PDF) —
978-1-4965-3155-1 (reflowable epub)

Summary: Ellie can't wait to pair up with her best friend,
Hannah, for a school Earth Day project. But when the project
becomes more than her super skills can handle, Ellie uses
one of her parents' inventions to create a copy of herself.
When the copy threatens to take over the project, it's up to
the real Ellie to bring the project back down to earth.

Editor: Alison Deering
Designer: Hilary Wacholz

Printed in Canada.
010033S17

For Sofia and Milla, my heroes — love, Mom

Team Earth
Takeover

written by Gina Bellisario

illustrated by Jessika von Innerebner

STONE ARCH BOOKS
a capstone imprint

TABLE OF CONTENTS

CHAPTER 1

Ellie's Super Duty

It was just another day in the city of Winkopolis. Froggies croaked. Fishies swam. Friends played. Everyone was busy doing the same old, ordinary things. Everyone except for the girl who lived at 8 Louise Lane.

That girl was Ellie Ultra. She was bouncing in her seat at Winkopolis Elementary School, higher than a rabbit on super-powered springs. It was *extraordinary*.

"My goodness, Ellie!" her teacher, Miss Little, exclaimed. "You're as hoppity as a snowshoe hare. Would you like to give your animal and habitat report next?"

"Yes!" Ellie shouted. Jumping to her feet, she whisked the report off her desk. Then she flew toward the front of the room.

Owen, one of Ellie's classmates, had just finished giving his report about the pancake tortoise. As he took a bow, Ellie flew past, accidentally knocking him over.

"Hold your horses!" Owen said, rubbing his bottom.

"Sorry!" Ellie said. She flexed her muscle power and scooped Owen up in her arms. Then she returned him safely to his seat.

Ellie quickly took her place in front of the rest of the third-grade class. She was eager to talk about her topic — the golden-cheeked warbler.

The bird was nearly extinct, and Ellie was determined to save it. After all, she was a superhero. Saving things was her specialty!

"The golden-cheeked warbler is a small bird with yellow cheeks," Ellie began. "It lives in the forest, where there are trees and shrubs and other brush. The warbler eats insects and pieces of nuts. But it's endangered. Too many trees are being cut down."

Ellie paused and looked at her classmates. "Not by Ax the Lumberjack. I stopped that villain when he tried to chop down my tree house. Humans are the ones cutting them down!"

At his desk, Ellie's classmate Dex was drawing a picture of her in his notebook. He made her look like a tree, with branches for arms and legs. Ax the Lumberjack was chasing her.

"Timberrrr!" Dex whispered so that Miss Little couldn't hear. But Ellie's powerful ears picked up his voice loud and clear.

Ellie narrowed her eyes. She was sure Dex was secretly an evil mastermind. *He's peskier than a hoverfly,* she thought.

"Thank you for your report, Ellie," Miss Little said as Ellie sat back down. "Trees are removed to build houses and roads. Even schools like ours. But cutting them down can hurt the environment. There are other things that also cause problems for our planet. Can anyone give an example?"

Joshua raised his hand. "If you forget to turn off the lights, you're wasting electricity."

"Don't throw away cans and plastic cups," Amanda added. "That stuff can be recycled."

Across the room, Payton held up her key chain, which was made out of a plastic bottle cap. The cap was painted like a soccer ball. "I turned a plastic bottle cap into this key chain," she said. "It's called *upcycling.*"

Ellie's hand shot up. "Miss Little, I can fight the planet's problems," she said confidently. "I took care of Electro Pig last week. That super-villain is the biggest energy hog in Winkopolis. But the Litter Bug is still dropping candy wrappers around school. I'll catch that critter creep, though. Superhero's honor!"

"I know Ellie Ultra can save the world," Miss Little replied. "But the planet is everyone's habitat. We all share that responsibility. In fact, that brings us to next week's assignment."

The teacher grabbed a stack of papers and handed them out to the class. "Next week is Earth Week. To celebrate, we're going to team up to help Earth!"

Ellie eagerly examined the paper. It read:

Team up for Earth Week! You and a partner will work on a project that helps the environment. Team projects will go on display during our classroom's Earth Day Showcase.

"Our showcase is next Friday — Earth Day," Miss Little explained. "We'll start working on and setting up our projects Monday. You'll have the weekend to get started on them. What do you say, class? Do you want to team up and help our planet?"

"Yeah!" the students answered excitedly.

Everybody started to pair up. Joshua and Owen bumped fists. Payton and Amanda pointed at each other and giggled.

As the rest of the class got into teams, Ellie sat quietly. She always saved Earth by herself. Why should she ask for help? Just then, she felt a tug on her cape and turned.

Waving at Ellie from the next row was her best friend, Hannah. If Ellie had to team up with somebody, she would choose Hannah in a super heartbeat.

"Hey, teammate!" Hannah squealed. "I already have an idea for our project. How about we make garbage that disappears? Poof! No more litter!"

"Sure!" Ellie replied. She knew she could save the world on her own, but she would take on any project as long as it helped the planet. It was her super duty!

CHAPTER 2

Sharing the Planet

At recess, everyone went outside. Usually, Ellie played Superhero Flight School on the swings with Hannah. But today, she had volunteered for Litter Patrol on the playground. Miss Little had picked Hannah to help too, even though Ellie didn't really need a hand — at least she wouldn't if the plastic patrol gloves fit better.

Ellie tugged at the gloves to keep them from falling off. "Oops!" she said as a juice box slipped through her fingers. The box fell onto the basketball court, and some yellow juice dribbled out.

"Eww, garbage is so gross!" Hannah said, scooping it into the trash bag. She watched as Ellie fumbled with the finger holes. "Need some help?"

"No, I can handle it," Ellie replied quickly. "Saving the world is what I do." She took off the gloves and whipped herself into a whirlwind. Chip bags, straws, and napkins sailed off the ground.

"Hey!" Dex shouted as a basketball flew from his hands.

Ellie's vortex sucked up the objects, including the basketball. She spun over a garbage can and stopped. *FWUMP!* Everything fell into the barrel.

"See? No help needed!" Ellie said, a little out of breath.

Turning up his nose, Dex dug his basketball out of the garbage. The ball smelled like hot lunch leftovers. "Your help *stinks!*" he snapped at Ellie.

As Dex walked away, Hannah said, "Don't listen to him. You did a great job. Of course, I could've helped . . ." She glanced around. "But now the playground is nice and clean."

"It's the perfect habitat for kids," Ellie replied with a smile.

The playground had everything: a swing set, monkey bars, and a twisty slide. It even had a track where the students ran laps during gym class.

It was a shame the school grounds wouldn't make a good home for the golden-cheeked warbler. There weren't many trees — just a lonely oak outside Miss Little's classroom. The rest had probably been taken down when the school was built.

Ellie frowned. "The school should also have a place for animals. We share the planet with them, after all." Just then — *Ka-ZAP!* — a super thought struck her. "What if we make an animal habitat? It could be our project for the Earth Day Showcase!"

"I like that idea! Much easier than making garbage disappear." Hannah scratched her head. "But where?"

"Let's ask Miss Little!" Ellie suggested. She and Hannah raced inside. In Room #128, their teacher was unrolling an Earth Day poster. "Miss Little, guess what?" Ellie said. "For our project, we decided to make a home for animals right here at school!"

"Wonderful!" Miss Little exclaimed. "That's called a schoolyard habitat. It's a place where animals can live and students can learn about them." She walked over to the window and motioned to the oak tree outside. "Animals need shelter, so you can build the habitat under that tree. They also need water and food."

Hannah turned to Ellie. "We have our project," she said. "Now what should we call our team? Team Earth?"

Ellie nodded agreeably. She'd been thinking of something more superhero-y — like Planet Protectors of Awesomeness — but Team Earth would do.

"Go, Team Earth!" Hannah said, tossing her hand up.

Ellie high-fived Hannah. She couldn't wait to start their project. She was going to save the planet or her super name wasn't Ellie Ultra!

CHAPTER 3

Two of a Kind

Creating a habitat was sort of like fighting a super-villain — Team Earth needed to create a plan of attack. So on Saturday, Hannah came over with her notebook to do just that.

They headed upstairs to Ellie's room right away. It was a super place to think. A poster of Ellie's favorite character, Princess Power, hung on the wall. She also had loads of comic books filled with the best planet-protecting ideas.

As Ellie's trusted canine sidekick, Super Fluffy, chased his toy soccer ball, Hannah turned to a new page in her notebook. She wrote *Team Earth To-Do List* at the top of the page. Then they set out making a list of jobs to complete their project.

"First we need to dig out a space for the habitat," Hannah said. "That means we'll need a shovel. If we're going to plant stuff, we better bring other gardening tools too."

"Miss Little said animals need shelter, food, and water," Ellie added. "Birds can use the oak tree for shelter. But there should be a brush pile for rabbits and chipmunks."

"Those animals eat flowers. Let's plant different kinds of flowers for them. And for water, we can put in a birdbath! My mom probably has an old saucer we can use."

"Great!" Ellie agreed.

Hannah jotted down their ideas and held out the list. "Did we leave anything out?"

Ellie peered at the paper. It read:

Team Earth To-Do List

- *Bring a shovel to dig out a space. Don't forget gardening tools!*

- *Gather sticks and leaves. Make a brush pile.*

- *Plant all sorts of flowers for food.*

- *Find a saucer and put in a birdbath. Fill the birdbath with fresh water.*

"Can you add one last thing? It's super important," Ellie said. "I want to build a birdhouse — a home for the golden-cheeked warbler!"

"Got it." Hannah added *Build a birdhouse* to the list. Then she tore out the page. "Now let's split up the jobs. If you collect twigs, I can make the brush pile —"

Before she could finish, Ellie snatched the list away.

"Hey, what are you doing?" Hannah asked.

"I'll take that job," Ellie said eagerly. "I can plant everything too. I'll plant tulips and sunflowers but no fire-breathing snapdragons. I'm not the wicked Garden Wizard." She giggled to herself.

Hannah looked puzzled. "You'll make a birdhouse and brush pile and plant stuff? That's a ton of work. I should help. We're a team."

"Oh, no, I won't need help!" Ellie replied. "Rescuing the planet is what I'm *supposed* to do. I'm the superhero, after all."

Hannah stared uneasily at Ellie. "If you say so," she finally said. "But I'll find something to make the birdbath, okay?" She glanced at the Princess Power clock hanging on Ellie's wall and closed her notebook. "My ballet class starts soon. I better go."

Once Hannah was gone, Ellie looked over the to-do list again. It *was* a ton of work, even for a third-grade superhero. But saving the world was her job, right?

Suddenly, her stomach grumbled. *I can't save Earth on an empty super stomach*, Ellie thought. She flew into the kitchen and poked around the pantry.

"Hi, Ellie!" her dad's voice said, only it sounded like two voices coming from one Dad.

Ellie turned curiously. There was Dad, side-by-side with . . . himself! Ellie's mouth fell open. "Dad!" she shouted. "You're doubled!"

Ellie knew her dad was one-of-a-kind. Who else built super-genius gadgets for B.R.A.I.N., a super-villain-fighting group? The only other person who did that was Mom. But if Dad was so one-of-a-kind, why were there *two* of him?

One of the dads stepped forward and winked at Ellie. "That's right. I made a copy of myself, but I'm the original."

"How did you do that?" Ellie asked.

Dad plucked a small ring out of his lab coat. On top of the ring was a glowing orange button. "I used the Ultra Copy Button," he replied. "It's our latest invention."

"The Ultra Copy Button?" Ellie repeated. "Can I try?"

Dad slipped the Ultra Copy Button on Ellie's finger. The button faced palm-side up. "To make a copy appear, give yourself a high-five," he explained. "To make the copy disappear, give your copy a high-five. Understand?"

Ellie nodded. She raised her hands and gave them a mighty *CLAP!* The button flashed, and a new Ellie appeared!

"Twin heroes!" Ellie said, standing proudly next to her clone. "Just think of how many bad guys we could bust." She turned to her copy and raised her hand. "Go, Ellie Ultras!"

CLAP! The button flashed again, and Ellie #2 was gone. Ellie handed the invention back to her dad.

"Handy gadget, isn't it?" Dad said. "Since Mom's away at the B.R.A.I.N. Invention Convention until Friday, I needed help finishing the Ultra Soaker." He motioned to the device his copy was holding.

The Ultra Soaker was another of Mr. and Mrs. Ultra's latest inventions. It might've looked like an ordinary hose, but one squirt could fill a swimming pool.

On the end of the soaker there was a large suction cup that sucked moisture out of the air. Then the soaker turned it into water, which sprayed

out through a nozzle. It had three speeds: *Bath time,*
Where's the fire? and *WIPE OUT!*

Dad #2 pulled out a lever that read *Rain, Rain,*
Go Away from his pocket. Ellie figured it turned
the invention off. After screwing the lever onto the
nozzle, the copy said, "The Ultra Soaker is all done.
I'll put it away."

Dad and Ellie watched as Dad #2 hurried
downstairs to the underground laboratory. "I sure
make a helpful partner," Dad said, grinning. "That
reminds me. How's the project coming along with
Hannah?"

"Great! We came up with a to-do list." Standing
tall, Ellie handed it over.

"Popping plasma!" Dad raised his eyebrows.
"That's a lot to do! Good thing you have Hannah's
help."

"Yeah, I guess," Ellie replied, shrinking a little.

First Hannah had thought Ellie needed help. Now Dad did too. Obviously, they didn't understand. It was *Ellie's* responsibility to save Earth — all by her super self.

CHAPTER 4

How Can I Save You?

The next day, Ellie peeked into the backyard shed. It was as spooky as a super-villain's lair. The whole thing was filled with darkness and forked things and — *gasp!* — cobwebs.

"Spiders!" Ellie said, trembling. The thought of them gave her the creeps. Spiders were worse than a vampire bat.

Spiders or no spiders, I need supplies for the schoolyard habitat, she thought. *Tomorrow is the first day of Earth Week. I have to get started on my project.*

Blinking on her X-ray vision, Ellie scanned the shed for eight-legged foes. Her eyebeams crossed over a wheelbarrow, then snaked around shelves. They finally stopped on a rolled-up sow bug.

Ellie breathed a sigh of relief. "All clear."

While Super Fluffy held the to-do list, Ellie gathered supplies. She grabbed seeds, potting soil, and tulip bulbs. Comet-quick, she collected everything but the garden sink.

"Uh-oh!" Ellie suddenly exclaimed. "I forgot a shovel."

She shuffled toward the wall, a tower of tools swaying in her arms. Just then, a small spider crawled out of the handle. It skittered up the pole, moving closer and closer toward Ellie's hand.

"SPIDER!" Ellie screeched. She tossed her arms into the air. Bags, bulbs, and the rest of the supplies flew everywhere.

CLUNK! CLUNK! CLUNK! They rained down as Ellie and Super Fluffy bolted out of the shed.

Racing past Dad's anti-gravity tomato plants, Ellie escaped into the house. "Phew!" she said, sighing with relief. "Safe from that evil arachnid and its fearsome fangs of terror!"

Confused, Super Fluffy tilted his head. He didn't seem to understand Ellie's panic. He thought the spider had seemed rather ordinary.

"Okay, maybe the spider wasn't *totally* evil," Ellie admitted. But still, she didn't want to be anywhere near it.

After smoothing her cape, Ellie read the to-do list carefully: *Dig out a space. Make a brush pile. Plant all sorts of flowers.*

While she read, each responsibility piled onto her super shoulders. It felt as heavy as a blue whale.

Ellie realized she couldn't carry the whole project by herself. If she was going to save the world, she really did need help.

Super Fluffy cast a look at Ellie. "I know what you're thinking, Fluffster," Ellie said. "I should split the work with Hannah. She's my partner, and it's a team project. But this project is about rescuing Earth. A superhero can't ask for help doing that. It's cuckoo bananas!"

Ellie plopped down at the kitchen table to think. How could she do the project alone? It was too much work for one superhero. If only there were two of her.

Suddenly, an orange glow caught Ellie's super eye. On the table was the Ultra Copy Button.

"If Dad can use the button to help finish a project, why can't I do the same?" Ellie wondered aloud. "I can make another Ellie to share the work. Then I'd save the day all by myself, exactly like a superhero should!"

Ellie stuffed the invention into her pocket. She was extra proud of her brilliant brainstorm. The project was no match for Ellie Ultra — times two!

* * *

That night, Ellie video-chatted with Mom on the Ultra Face-to-Face Phone. She wanted to share her do-gooding deed for Earth Day.

"I'm making a schoolyard habitat," Ellie told her mom. "It's for our classroom's Earth Day Showcase. Families can come see it. Will you get home in time?"

"I hope so," Mom replied onscreen. "In the meantime, happy planting! Just don't plant any cornflowers, okay? They'll attract zombie groundhogs."

"Okay," Ellie agreed. She puckered up and blew Mom a kiss goodbye. Then she handed the phone to Dad and flew to her room.

After finishing homework, Ellie pulled out the Ultra Copy Button. It glowed brightly on her finger. She clapped her hands, pressing the button, and . . . *FLASH!* Ellie #2 appeared!

The copy stood before Ellie, ready for action. "Ellie Ultra at your super service!" she said excitedly. "How can I save you?"

Wow, I'm all set to help out, Ellie thought. *How super of me!*

Ellie stuck out her hand. "Nice to meet you, Ellie," she replied. "I'm the original Ellie. I got myself into a bit of a mess. That's where you come in. With your help, I can clean up everything!"

"Everything?" Ellie #2 echoed. Her eyes darted from the floor to the bookshelf. "Consider it done!"

Like a firecracker, the copy exploded into the air and zoomed out of the room. Instantly she returned with a broom and a dust cloth. She swept Ellie's floor. She dusted Ellie's bookshelf.

Ellie watched in amazement as her clone put her entire comic book collection — from *Astro Ant* to the *Zombie-Eating Pumpkin* — in order.

Just then Super Fluffy bounded into the room. He had been playing outside, and his hair was a messy mop.

"Yikes! That dog needs a bath!" Ellie #2 said. Without waiting for a response, she whisked him off to the bathroom. Moments later, she brought back a sparkling clean Super Fluffy.

Ellie's copy tied a pretty bow on his head. Super Fluffy just stared helplessly at his original owner.

"Whoa, Ellie!" Ellie exclaimed, coming to her pup's rescue. "I didn't mean for you to clean my room — or my dog. I need help with a team project at school." She handed over the to-do list.

Ellie #2 scanned the list up and down. "Plant flowers? Make a brush pile? Sure! I can do that. No super sweat."

Ellie smiled. "I bet you can do everything — single-handedly!" She high-fived Ellie #2, being careful not to erase her copy with the Ultra Copy Button. After all, the planet needed them!

"Go, Team Earth!" Ellie cheered.

CHAPTER 5

Hero Gone Wild

Before school on Monday, Ellie #2 got a head start on the to-do list. She'd spent the night before gathering gardening tools in the shed. She was still at work when Ellie flew down for breakfast.

Peeking out the kitchen window, Ellie saw her copy loading the tools into a wheelbarrow. *What a super partner!* she thought.

Ellie wanted to help, but first, she needed food power. She headed to the table, where a plate of food awaited.

Dad held up the frying pan. "More sausage?" he asked.

"Mesh, pweesh!" Ellie mumbled through a mouthful of eggs. She finished chewing and swallowed. "Yes, please!"

Dad filled her plate. "Are you excited to work on your Earth Week project at school today?" he asked.

"Yes!" Ellie exclaimed. "Did you know two thousand trees are cut down every minute? If people don't save forests, there will be none left in a hundred years!"

"None?" Dad repeated.

"Uh-huh! And did you know most animals live in forests? That's hundreds of species! They could all become extinct."

Dad's forehead wrinkled. "Our world needs more superheroes," he said. "At least you're doing your part. Did you get all the supplies for your project?"

Ellie was about to answer when the back door banged shut. Seconds later, the wheelbarrow rolled into the kitchen. Inside were trowels, rakes, a watering can, and just about every other gardening tool in the galaxy.

Ellie #2 appeared from behind a stack of clay pots. "I'm ready to start," she said. "I'll knock out the list with a *WHAM!* And a *SMASH!* And a *CRUNCH!*"

Dad turned from Ellie to Ellie's copy to Ellie again. "That's funny," he said. "I thought I had only one super daughter."

"I copied myself," Ellie explained proudly. "I needed an extra hand with the habitat. Is that okay?"

"Since you used the Ultra Copy Button for good, I suppose so," Dad replied. "But don't you already have a partner? What about Hannah?"

Ellie shrugged. "Two super partners are better than one, right?"

"I guess you're right." Dad glanced over at Ellie #2, who was busy sorting seeds into pots. "Your copy is taking her job seriously."

"Saving the world is serious business!" Ellie said. She finished eating and hopped up from the table. She grabbed her homework and backpack and reached for the wheelbarrow.

Suddenly Ellie #2 sprang in front of her. "Stand back, Ellie!" the copy said. "I'll carry the tools. That's what I'm here for!"

Ellie raised her eyebrows. The copy was taking her job super seriously! But she *was* being helpful — and that's why Ellie had created her in the first place.

"Uh, thanks," Ellie replied as Ellie #2 hurried away with the heavy load. She threw on her cape and headed for the door. "Bye, Dad!"

"Bye, Dad!" Ellie #2 echoed.

Dad waved from the doorway. "Um, bye, Ellies!"

* * *

As soon as they arrived at school, Ellie #2 wheeled the supplies to the oak tree. Ellie figured it was for the best. She would hardly be able to cram everything into her locker. Even with super strength.

While her copy unloaded everything from soil to spades, Ellie hurried inside before the bell rang. "Leaping ring-tailed lemurs!" she exclaimed when she entered the classroom.

Room #128 had gone wild for Earth Week. The walls were covered with pictures of the animals the class had discussed in their reports. There was a sea lion. There was a red wolf. And above Miss Little's desk hung a picture of Ellie's topic, the golden-cheeked warbler.

Miss Little had also taped up posters that showed how to help the environment. They were full of suggestions like: *Recycle. Plant trees. Turn off faucets. Walk.*

If everyone did those things, the world wouldn't need any superheroes, Ellie thought. *Well, unless there's an invasion of mutant earthworms.*

Just then, she felt someone tap her shoulder. It was probably Ellie #2 saying she'd finished already. But when she turned around, Hannah popped up instead.

"Ellie! Guess what I made for us to wear at the showcase?" Hannah said. She held up a T-shirt with a picture of two stick figures hugging the planet. One figure had Ellie's dark curls, and the other had Hannah's straight dark hair. "Official Team Earth shirts!"

Ellie smiled. "That's us."

"Right!" Hannah replied. "Since you offered to tackle the to-do list, I had free time this weekend. So I made a shirt for each of us. We're already a team, but now we can look like one too!"

Out of nowhere, Ellie #2 swooped in and snatched the shirt away from Hannah. "Super-cool shirt!" she said, putting it on. "Thanks!"

One look at Ellie's copy, and Hannah turned as pale as a ghost. "Ellie? Is that . . . *you?*"

"It's a *copy* of me," Ellie quickly explained. "I made Ellie with my parents' latest invention, the Ultra Copy Button. I have a lot to do for the project, so she's here to lend a hand."

"Um, *hello?*" Hannah waved her hands around. "I have *two* hands. I know I can't lift a rhino or melt a spoon like you can, but I can still help. Why didn't you ask me? We're teammates!"

Ellie was quiet for a minute. If she wasn't a superhero, she would've asked. But she was super enough for this task. It was no different than fighting Ax the Lumberjack.

"I have everything under control," Ellie replied.

"Oh, really?" Hannah pointed to the recycling bin. "Then why is the other Ellie throwing away your homework?"

"My what?" Ellie whipped around. Sure enough, Ellie #2 was dangling her homework above the recycling bin.

"Wait! Stop!" Ellie hollered. Her fiery feet burned through the classroom. She swiped the worksheet away, saving it from environmentally friendly doom. "What are you doing?"

"Helping, silly," the copy replied. "I'll take care of the project outside, but what about in here? I can do a TON! I can recycle paper, change light bulbs, fight germs . . ." She held up a face mask and a bottle of hand sanitizer. "And that's just for starters!"

Ellie doubted Miss Little would be happy to find a superhero running amok in the classroom. "Why don't you wait by the oak tree until we're ready to build the habitat?" she suggested gently, putting her arm around the copy and steering her toward the door. "Please?"

Ellie #2 looked disappointed. But after a moment, she replied, "Okay. But call if you need anything. A pencil sharpened. A math quiz defeated. Anything."

As she watched her copy head back outside, Ellie grew a little worried. Ellie #2 was helpful . . . but was there such a thing as *too* helpful?

CHAPTER 6

Not-So-Super Helper

Ellie #2 had to wait until science to help with the project. That meant original Ellie spent most of the morning trying to keep track of her double out the window.

Unfortunately Ellie #2 wasn't staying under the oak tree like Ellie had asked. During Share Time, she set up a car wash in the teachers' parking lot.

During reading, she decorated the school sign, adding streamers and glitter.

Ellie glanced away from the window to write *The Zombie-Eating Pumpkin: Eyeball Snack Attack!* in her reading log. When she looked up again, her copy was gone.

What's that do-gooder up to? she wondered. *Fetching overdue library books? Mopping the cafeteria?*

The copy had to come back. If Ellie #2 didn't help with the project, Ellie wouldn't be able to finish everything. The showcase was only days away. She couldn't let down Team Earth! Especially after she'd told Hannah she had it under control.

Just then, Miss Little rang the class wind chime to get everyone's attention. "Science time!" she announced. "Teams, gather the supplies you'll need for your Earth Week projects. Let's work together to help our planet!"

All the students hurried to their lockers. Joshua and Owen were the first ones back. They now had a box of pencils, glue, and glow-in-the-dark shoelaces. After spreading out their supplies on the rug, they got started. Joshua put glue on a pencil. Then Owen wrapped the pencil in a shoelace.

Miss Little peeked over at them. "What are you making?" she asked.

"Light-up pencils!" Joshua replied. "You can use them to do homework at night. That way you'll save electricity." He thought for a second. "Or teachers could just stop assigning homework."

"Miss Little?" Amanda piped up. "Can Payton and I get plastic bottles from the cafeteria? For our project, we're turning bottles into art caddies!"

The teacher nodded, and the girls skipped off with a bag. As Amanda and Payton rushed past, Ellie leaped from her seat. She hurried toward the window, hoping to spot Ellie #2 outside. But glancing around the grounds left her with a frown on her face.

"Not a superhero in sight," Ellie said with a sigh.

"Back off, Super Smelly!" Dex said. He shooed Ellie away from his desk. "This is a No-Superhero Zone!" He was working by himself and poking holes in a shocbox.

It figures, Ellie thought. Evil masterminds usually worked alone, unless they had minions doing their dirty deeds.

Ellie stepped back, carefully scanning the other supplies on Dex's desk. She expected a mind control helmet or something equally evil. But all she saw were acorns, soil, and a bottle of GroDream plant food.

Ellie's eyes widened as it hit her — Dex was growing mutant tree minions!

She got ready to sound an alarm, but before she could, Hannah yanked her toward the door.

"C'mon, Ellie!" she said. "Our habitat's waiting for us outside."

"Too bad my copy isn't," Ellie muttered to herself. Where was a superhero when you needed one?

* * *

In the shade of the oak tree, Hannah picked through Ellie's shovels and pots. "You're sure prepared!" she exclaimed. "I better collect my supplies. I need leaves to decorate the birdbath." She grabbed her backpack and ran around the corner. "Call me if you need help!"

"Did somebody say *help*?" Ellie #2 swooped down in front of Ellie. "I can do that!"

"Where were you?" Ellie demanded, relieved her copy had returned. "And what were you doing?"

"Helping the citizens of Winkopolis," Ellie #2 replied. "I carried bags at the grocery store. Then I picked thorns off the neighbor's rose bush. Oh! And

I did something extra helpful at the Wacky World Museum."

Ellie loved the Wacky World Museum. It had lots of cool stuff, including caveman teeth and a jellybean portrait of Wink Binkerton, the founding father of Winkopolis.

"How did you help?" Ellie asked.

"One room was *really* dirty," Ellie #2 explained. "There was a giant ball of dust that somebody forgot to clean it up. I threw it away. But the guard didn't look too happy."

"That was the World's Biggest Dust Bunny!" Ellie hollered. "It took years to make!"

"Oops." Ellie #2 shrugged. "No need to worry! I'll make a new one!"

Ellie sighed. "I think you've helped enough. Besides, we need to start the habitat. Do you have the to-do list?"

"Do superheroes save the day? Of course I have it!" Ellie #2 whipped out the list and scanned it. "The first thing is to clear a space."

Ellie surveyed the land. There was enough room to make a home for hundreds of crawling critters and feathery friends. But Miss Little had suggested keeping the habitat small. After all, Team Earth only had until Friday to finish everything.

"Okay, let's get to work," Ellie said. After sweeping up some twigs, she placed them around the oak, creating a small circle. "The habitat should fit inside this space," she told her copy. "How about you clear out half of the grass, and I'll clear out the other half?"

Ellie bent over the wheelbarrow to grab two shovels. Suddenly, she heard a terrible *RIIIIP!* Looking up, she saw her copy holding a huge roll of grass in one hand.

"Space cleared? Check!" Ellie #2 said proudly. Behind her, a rectangle — twice the size of the space Ellie had wanted — had been torn out.

"This space is too big!" Ellie cried. "It looks like a herd of hungry robo-cows were grazing here!"

Ellie #2 shrugged. "The bigger the better! After I clean up the grass, I'll start the next job!" She threw the grass on her shoulder and flew off.

Just then, Hannah ran over. Leaves fell out of her backpack. "I saw what your copy did," she said. "Don't you think she went a little . . . overboard?"

The copy had made a super-sized mistake, but Ellie couldn't tell Hannah that. Hannah might think that Ellie couldn't handle her job. And everyone knew superheroes did things on their own.

Ellie simply pasted on a smile and replied, "The bigger the better! I think she's doing a super job. Go, Team Earth!"

CHAPTER 7

Junkyard Blues

On Tuesday, science started off rocky. Ellie had just begun working on the habitat when an enormous boulder came rolling toward her. She was about to become a human bowling pin!

"Yikes!" Ellie yelped. At the last minute, she zipped into the air, landing safely under the oak tree. "Whew! I was almost a super pancake!"

"Are you okay, Ellie?" Hannah asked, hurrying over. She looked very worried.

"Watch out!" Ellie #2 called as another rock rolled past. "Here comes the world's biggest brush pile!"

With a power-packed push, the copy sent the boulder flying to the edge of the clearing. It crashed into a pair of sneakers.

"ROCK AND ROOOLLL!" Ellie #2 belted out, playing an air guitar.

Hannah leaned over to original Ellie. "Brush pile?" she whispered. "Looks more like a junkyard."

Ellie nodded. Her copy had started to build the brush pile, which was next on the to-do list. It should've been made out of branches and twigs where small animals could find shelter.

But Ellie #2 had stacked anything she could find — an old basketball net, hats from the lost-and-found box, and Miss Little's coffee mug — into a massive mound.

Hannah picked up some branches. "What are you doing?" Ellie asked.

"I'll help you make the brush pile," Hannah replied. "Your copy is busy with her own . . . uh . . . project."

"I don't need help! Cross my cape." Ellie swung her cape around and made an X. "It's my job, remember? I said I'd do that stuff on the list. So I will."

Hannah took a long and noisy breath. "Fine," she said at last. "But it's *our* project, you know. I'd like to help too." She plopped down next to her backpack and stewed.

Ellie floated away quietly. She knew Hannah wanted to split up the work. Her super mind-reading power told her that. But she wouldn't ask her friend to fight a saber-toothed hamster. Why would this be any different?

When Ellie reached the pile, she noticed her copy was standing on a surfboard. "Cowabunga, Dudette!" Ellie #2 said, hanging ten. "Look what I found in the principal's office!"

"Mr. Cleveland surfs?" Ellie asked. "I didn't know that. I thought principals only did principal things, like tell goofy jokes."

"That's funny. I thought so too!" Ellie's copy hopped down. "I'm going to add this to the pile. Mr. Cleveland probably won't mind."

Ellie wasn't so sure about that. Besides, a brush pile was supposed to be a pile of brush — not sporting gear. "Why don't you add branches and leaves instead?" she suggested.

"Leaves? Super idea!" X-ray beams shot out of Ellie #2's eyes and scanned the playground. When they reached Hannah's backpack, the beams stopped and flickered.

Quick as a flash, Ellie #2 flew to where Hannah sat and snatched the backpack. Then she swooped over to the brush pile and shook out every last leaf Hannah had collected to decorate the birdbath.

"Off to get one last thing!" the copy announced. She raced across the baseball diamond and disappeared in a whirlwind of dust. The gust of wind she left behind swept in and blew the leaves away.

"Thanks for your *help*," Hannah muttered, glaring at Ellie. Then she stormed off to gather more leaves.

Ellie moved to follow Hannah — she knew she needed to apologize — when a long shadow passed overhead. Then there came an earth-shaking *CRRRAASH!*

"All done!" Ellie #2 sang. She beamed at the brush pile. A tree now teetered like a seesaw on top. It had been pulled straight out of the ground, and its roots dangled limply.

"What did you *do*?" Ellie hollered.

"You told me to add branches," Ellie #2 said. "So I got a tree. Does this tree have enough branches? If not, I can bring another one."

Ellie was horrified. Her copy, planet protector and super-good Earthling, had toppled a tree faster than Ax the Lumberjack! Hopefully, Hannah hadn't noticed.

She glanced over and saw Hannah staring at the tree. No such luck. Hannah shook her head slowly and walked away.

Ellie threw her hands up. "No more trees, please!" she begged.

"Okay, okay!" Ellie #2 pulled out the to-do list. "Since I'm finished, I'll start planting flowers." She dashed over to the wheelbarrow and grabbed a trowel. "Go, planting power!"

Ellie turned her attention to the brush pile. She didn't want to take her eyes off her copy, but science was almost over. She needed to return everyone's stuff — especially the principal's surfboard.

But what about the tree? Ellie wondered. Her gaze fell on the hunk of wood. It could've been home to an animal, even the golden-cheeked warbler. *If only I could return that.*

After rolling up her sleeves, Ellie set to picking the pile apart. She pulled out a mop, then a jump rope. As she unplugged a toilet plunger — *KA-POOEY!* — a foul odor struck her nose. It smelled like a musk ox. Or a stink bird.

"Yuckola!" Ellie exclaimed. "What is that?"

Suddenly, Ellie #2 held up a handful of eye-stinging onions. "Guess what I'm making?"

"Toxic waste?" Ellie asked, waving the smell away.

"Wrong! It's a compost heap." Ellie #2 stepped aside and revealed a mountain of eggshells, apple cores, and pizza crusts. "If I'm going to grow flowers,

I need plant food — super plant food! I hope flowers like onions."

Ellie stared at the heap. It oozed oatmeal. It spewed sawdust. It gushed green and goopy and gloppy goo that reminded her of a certain super-villainous blob.

"My help *stinks*," she muttered, catching a whiff of old bananas.

The mess was enough to make Ellie want to erase her copy. She wondered if Team Earth was better off without Ellie #2's help.

But if Ellie erased her copy, the project would fall entirely on her shoulders again. And Ellie #2 was only trying to help. That had to count for something. Maybe the copy deserved one more chance . . . after all, what was the worst a superhero could do?

CHAPTER 8

Swamped

At school on Wednesday, Ellie held her breath during reading. The classroom reeked like a tuna-and-toxic-waste sandwich. But Ellie knew what was really responsible for the smell — the compost heap decaying outside.

Saving the world is a stinky job, Ellie thought.

When it was time for science, the teams continued to work on their projects. Ellie helped Joshua empty the classroom recycling bin. Then it was time to meet Hannah at the oak tree. But since the air was chilly, she needed to get her cape first.

A frosty glare hit Ellie as she closed her locker. "Hannah!" she said, jumping back. "For a second, I thought you were the Ice Queen. Her look is so cold, it can turn you into a Popsicle!"

"I know you don't want to hear this," Hannah said, "but your copy's superhero skills could use some work. Ellie #2 isn't helping our team."

Truthfully, Ellie knew Hannah was right. Ellie #2 was about as helpful as a wrecking ball. But it was Ellie's super duty to complete the list. She couldn't ask Hannah for help *now* — especially not after she'd made such a big deal about doing it on her own.

"What do you mean?" Ellie asked as if she didn't have mind-reading powers.

"First, she bulldozed the grass," Hannah said. She held up a finger to keep count. "Second, she piled up junk. Third, she made the classroom stinky. And what about this morning? Did you see all the flowers she planted?"

Before school, Ellie #2 had snuck over to add animal food to the habitat. She had planted enough tulips and sunflowers for every rabbit and chipmunk in the neighborhood.

"Maybe she's excited about helping?" Ellie offered.

"Excited? You can say that again. Look at what she did to my T-shirt!" Hannah held up her Team Earth T-shirt.

The stick figure of Hannah had been crossed out. So had the words *Team Earth*. In their place, Ellie #2 had written a new name — *Team Ellie*.

"Ellie isn't helping," Hannah finished. "She's taking over our project!"

Ellie could see that even without X-ray vision! "I'll take care of my copy," she replied. "Right now she's watering the flowers. She said they looked thirsty."

Ellie's dad had agreed to let them use the Ultra Soaker for their project. That way, all the plants would get enough to drink.

"Good luck with . . . yourself," Hannah said. Turning to leave, she added, "I have to get the birdbath I made. I'll meet you outside!"

As Hannah stomped off to her locker, Ellie thought about how she'd handle Ellie #2. She'd battled bots and tamed T-Rexes. But she'd never had to stop another superhero.

Just then, a pesky nose poked into the hallway. Ellie knew exactly who it belonged to — Dex Diggs, unstoppable master meanie.

"Hey, Ellie Ugh-tra!" he called. "I saw your animal home. Nice work."

Dex's words struck fear into Ellie's heart. Evil masterminds never said anything good. It was against the law of evil.

"What are you talking about, Dex?" she asked.

"Duh! Your habitat," Dex replied with a smirk. "It's seaweed soup! What will live there? A swamp monster?"

I wish Dex would go live in a swamp, Ellie thought.

Ignoring her pesky classmate was usually the best defense, but this time was different. A gut feeling — not to mention a quick peek at his mind — told Ellie something was off.

Breaking free from the mastermind, Ellie hurried outside to the oak tree. "Popping plasma!" she shouted when she saw their habitat.

Team Earth's project was underwater — literally! Tall, grassy leaves poked out of a murky pool. Frogs

belly-flopped while turtles snapped on the uprooted tree. At the edge, a long hose pumped gallons of water into the soaked space. It was the Ultra Soaker!

Ellie glanced around, but Ellie #2 was nowhere in sight. She had gone off and left the soaker running!

"The habitat's sunk!" Ellie cried.

Jumping into action, she grabbed the soaker and forced the nozzle skyward. The invention thrashed around like a grouchy sea serpent. It gurgled noisily and sprayed water every which way as Ellie fought to keep her grip.

Through sopping curls, Ellie noticed the speed on the nozzle. Her copy had set it to *WIPE OUT!*

"Oh, no!" she said with a gasp. "Ellie went overboard — again!"

Ellie knew she had to pull the plug on her copy's plan. Flying up, over, and through, she made a knot in the Ultra Soaker, tying off the water.

The soaker quieted down, except for a slurping sound coming from its suction cup. It was still sucking in water!

With nowhere to go, the water formed a bubble in the invention's long hose. It expanded wildly, stretching the soaker to the limits of stretchiness. The Ultra Soaker was about to explode!

Fast as a falcon, Ellie pulled the *Rain, Rain, Go Away* lever. But it was too late.

SPLOOOSH! The bubble popped, erupting into a tidal wave. The water shot toward the heavens, then sprinkled down like a soft spring shower.

Ellie wiped the rain from her eyes. "Dad's invention!" she exclaimed, staring at the hole in the Ultra Soaker. Dad would need a team of super-genius scientists to patch it.

Squish. Squish. Squish. Ellie's feet sloshed through the soggy clearing as she took in the damage.

There were limp leaves. There were mucky puddles. The habitat was a huge patch of mud. Worse than that, the odor from the compost heap hung in the air like P-U perfume.

"This isn't a good home for anything," Ellie muttered, avoiding a snapping turtle. "Not even for a swamp monster."

Ellie twirled into a tornado. After drying off, she planted herself on the uprooted tree to think.

How was she ever going to save Team Earth? Her copy had messed everything up. Now Ellie needed more help than ever.

CHAPTER 9

Water World

SPLAT!

Ellie #2 landed smack dab in the middle of
a puddle. She flashed a smile that would have
turned the evil dentist Dr. Pearly White — one of
Winkopolis' greatest super-villains — green with
envy. In her arms, flashing an even bigger smile, was
a crocodile!

"Check out what I got!" Ellie #2 stood tall, proudly holding the toothy beast. "A Nile crocodile! It's the first animal for my habitat. Next I'll bring a red-bellied water snake. Then a hairy woodpecker."

The crocodile wiggled loose. It was twice Ellie's size, with a belly that could fit a third-grade superhero easily.

Maybe it's a vegetarian like Cyclops, Ellie hoped. Her family's giant, one-eyed pet iguana loved vegetables, so Ellie always shared hers at dinner.

To be safe, Ellie backed away as the crocodile lumbered past. It curled up by the oak tree. "Man-eating reptiles aren't allowed on the playground," she told her copy. "Why don't you stick to the to-do list?"

"To-do list? You mean this old thing?" Ellie #2 pulled out the list and tossed it onto the compost heap. "I won't need it anymore for my project."

"*Your* project?" Ellie was confused. "Who said it was *your* project?"

"You did, silly!" the copy replied. "In our room, remember? You said I could do everything — single-handedly!"

The evil arachnid. Dad and Dad. Super Fluffy's makeover. Memories of that day swirled in Ellie's super mind. She had said those very words. But she'd only been excited about having her copy to help her — she hadn't expected Ellie #2 to take over the project completely!

"I decided to make a wetland with the Ultra Soaker," Ellie #2 continued. "And not just at school. *My* habitat will cover the whole world. Imagine how many animals I'll save!" She swung her fist through the air. "*BAM!* Take that, eco-villains!"

Just then Ellie #2 spotted the hole in the Ultra Soaker. "Whoops! I must've turned it up too much."

As her copy examined the invention, Ellie sadly stared at her double. Her plan had been a bust. She should've let Hannah help from the start. Now, she really needed her partner. Ellie #2 was out of control. She wouldn't stop lending a hand, even if it meant a Team Earth takeover!

Thinking quickly, Ellie took the Ultra Copy Button out of her backpack and slipped it on her hand. She made sure the button was palm-side up.

"Ellie," she said, easing up to her copy. "Before you make a water world — er — wetland, I just want to tell you, you're great at saving the planet."

Her copy lowered the soaker. "You think so?" she said brightly. "Well, thanks! It's my job, you know."

"Yep, I know. And since you're doing a good job, you deserve a high-five." Ellie raised her hand. "How about it?"

Ellie #2 jumped up triumphantly. "Go, Team Ellie!" she shouted, high-fiving Ellie. The Ultra Copy Button glowed orange and — *FLASH!* — the copy was gone.

Ellie breathed a sigh of relief. "The world might need more superheroes," she said, "but one Ellie Ultra is enough." She put the button back into her bag.

Just then Hannah appeared. "AAAHH!" she howled like a howler monkey. She stared at the habitat in horror. "What happened here? Did a storm come through?"

Ellie smiled weakly. "Well, it *was* a force of nature," she said. "Only more powerful."

"Your copy, huh?" Hannah let out a groan. "I can't take any more of Ellie's help. Can she save another planet, please? Besides Earth?"

"You won't hear from her again," Ellie promised. "I only copied myself because I thought it was my job to save the world. But I took over the project instead. I wasn't being a good partner. I'm sorry."

"You don't have to do all the work," Hannah replied. "If we're going to help Earth, we should both pitch in. We share the world, so it's *our* job." She stopped. "Of course if a super-villain attacks, I'll let you handle everything."

"I like that plan," Ellie said. She went quiet for a moment. "So I have a favor to ask — can you help me finish our project?"

"I thought you'd never ask!" Hannah brushed some twigs off the supplies and pulled out two shovels. "Let's get started. We only have today and tomorrow, and then it's showcase time!"

* * *

Team Earth spent the rest of science rescuing the project. Ellie and Hannah shoveled compost into the wheelbarrow. Then Ellie wheeled everything away,

dumping it into the city compost center. Hannah raked up mud, and Ellie filled in the grass that her copy had ripped out.

"Where did you get that from?" Hannah asked as Ellie rolled out a new grassy rug.

"My backyard," Ellie replied. "But the grass will grow back. All I have to do is use the Ultra Green Thumb. That gadget can make anything grow, even a corpse flower!"

Next, Ellie flew all the way to the Nile River. She dropped off the crocodile, which tried to snack on her cape, and then returned to help Hannah build a brush pile.

The girls gathered sticks from the uprooted tree, and while Hannah stacked them up, Ellie made stumps out of the trunk. It was easy with a few karate chops.

Finally Hannah rolled up a stump and sat down. "Whew! Being a hero is exhausting!" she said.

"That's why I can't stay up late," Ellie replied. "Mom says do-gooders need a good night's sleep."

"Yeah." Hannah reached under the wheelbarrow and picked up the birdbath. "I still have to fill this. Too bad that hose is busted." She pointed to the Ultra Soaker.

Ellie bit her lip as Hannah picked up the soaker. "Uh, Hannah. You're better off using something else. Trust me."

"Why?" Hannah asked, fumbling with the lever. "The nozzle is wet, so it must work."

"Oh, it works, all right. It could fill that birdbath faster than a tidal wave."

Hannah froze. She let go of the lever and put the Ultra Soaker back down — very, *very* slowly. "On second thought, I'll use the drinking fountain."

CHAPTER 10

Friends and Archenemies

The next day during science, Ellie stuck her shovel in the ground. "We're done!" she cheered.

Hannah joined Ellie, and together they admired their teamwork. The schoolyard habitat was finished. It now had a flowerbed on one side of the oak tree and a brush pile on the other. It had stumps for a friendly gathering space. It also had Hannah's birdbath, which was full of fresh water.

Ellie skipped along the welcoming path of stepping stones, which ran through the habitat. "Let's check to make sure we didn't forget anything," she said, pulling out the to-do list. She had saved it from under a pile of peach pits.

Ellie scanned the list while crossing out what Team Earth had completed.

Team Earth To-Do List

- ~~*Bring a shovel to dig out a space. Don't forget gardening tools!*~~

- ~~*Gather sticks and leaves. Make a brush pile.*~~

- ~~*Plant all sorts of flowers for food.*~~

- ~~*Find a saucer and put in a birdbath. Fill the birdbath with fresh water.*~~

- *Build a birdhouse.*

When she reached the bottom of the list, Ellie's face fell.

"What's the matter?" Hannah asked. "Is it cyborg spinach? A teacher creature?"

Ellie shook her head. "Worse! I didn't make a birdhouse! How can I save the golden-cheeked warbler without a birdhouse? It needs a home."

"All we have left is some soil and a broken pot," Hannah said as she dug into the wheelbarrow. "Those supplies won't help us."

Ellie sank onto a stump. She felt mighty un-mighty. If only she had asked for help sooner instead of trying to do everything on her own. Through the classroom window, Ellie could see the other kids celebrating. They were having no trouble finishing their projects. All because they had helped each other.

"Help! That's it!" Ellie jumped up and twirled Hannah like a doll. "We can still save the day. We just need help!" She ran inside, pulling Hannah behind her. "Payton! Amanda!"

Behind a yarn ball, Payton's head popped up. "What's up?" she asked.

"It's an Earth Day emergency!" Ellie replied. "Do you have any extra bottles left over from your project?"

"Extra? Be right back!" Payton zigzagged through the class and disappeared out the door. Moments later, she came back with a bag overflowing with plastic bottles. "How's *this* for extra?"

"Amazing!" Ellie exclaimed happily.

"The cafeteria is Bottletopia!" Amanda told her. "We found enough bottles to make art caddies for the whole school." She handed one over. "Let us know if you want more."

"Thanks!" Ellie and Hannah raced to the rug, which was shaped like a map of the United States. On California, Joshua and Owen were gluing glow-in-the-dark shoelaces to their shoes.

"Where's your pencil project?" Ellie asked her classmates.

"We're done with that," Joshua said. He nodded at Illinois and Michigan. There, pencils were wrapped in every color of the shoelace rainbow.

"Now, we're making light-up clothes," Owen explained. "Shoes, pants, everything! If our clothes glowed, we wouldn't have to waste electricity. We'd be giant glow sticks!"

It was a bright idea. But when Ellie tried to imagine the boys as light bulbs of liberty, she could only think of Electro Pig. That power-hungry villain glowed brighter than the city's power grid, after he'd drained it. Then he'd let out a super-charged *BURRRRP!*

Ellie punched her palm. "Evildoers have no manners," she muttered.

"Huh?" Owen scrunched his eyebrows.

Ellie shook her head. "Sorry, never mind. Can we use one of your pencils? And a shoelace? We're building a birdhouse for our habitat."

"Sure." Owen crawled over the Rocky Mountains. He swung around with a pencil and a neon blue shoelace. "These okay?"

"Perfect!" Ellie said.

Team Earth hurried around the classroom getting help from more teams. When they were finished, the girls spread out the new supplies on Ellie's desk.

"The bottle can be a house, and this pencil will make a perch," Ellie said.

"What about food?" Hannah asked. "You said warblers eat nuts, right? Too bad the oak tree doesn't have acorns now."

Just then, as if by magic or a squirrel's acorn blaster, an acorn shot overhead. Ellie caught it in midair.

Out of nowhere, Dex appeared. All Earth Week long, he had been tending to his newly planted acorns, feeding them plenty of GroDream plant food and evil ideas. No doubt they were growing into big, strong, leafy minions!

"Hands off, Snatcher Girl!" Dex snapped, swiping the acorn away. "Keep your super cooties to yourself."

"I, um . . ." Ellie's voice faded as she saw some leftover acorns on Dex's seat. *Dex! Acorns!* The sudden thought nearly fried her brainpower. Her archenemy could help — yes, *help* — their team! All she had to do was ask.

Ellie took a deep breath. "Dex, I need a favor. Can you help?"

"Help? *You?*" Dex's face wrinkled like a raisin. "What should I do? Pretend you're invisible? Move to the opposite end of the universe?"

"Well, actually . . ."

"Wait, wait, I know!" Dex interrupted. "Stop superheroes for all eternity? Sure, I can do that."

Ellie frowned. Saving the world was hard. How come villains made it harder? "Can I have a few acorns?" she asked.

Dex hopped over to his desk and returned with the acorns. Holding them out, he said, "I'll give you these. But first, you have to say, 'Evil masterminds are more super than superheroes.'" He started to juggle.

I'm getting nowhere with Dex, Ellie thought, watching the acorns go round and round. She needed someone powerful — more powerful than her, Mom and Dad, and all the members of B.R.A.I.N. put together — to ask him to help.

Just then, the answer to Ellie's prayers — Miss Little — walked up. "Is everything okay here?" she asked.

"We need acorns for our project," Ellie explained. "But Dex won't give us any, being my archenemy and all."

Miss Little turned to Dex. "Earth could use our help," she said. "We can do the most by working as a team. Girls and boys. Kids and grownups. Students and teachers. Friends *and* archenemies."

Dex stuck out his tongue at Ellie.

"C'mon, Dex," Miss Little said with a friendly nudge. "Earth is counting on you."

Time stood still as Dex thought quietly. From what Ellie mind-read, he was trying to decide between doing the right thing and the wrong thing. It looked like two toddlers fighting over a shiny balloon. But finally, he handed over the acorns — even super-villains had to listen to their teachers.

"Thanks, Dex!" Ellie said cheerfully. "I thought bad guys never helped good guys. But you've changed that. Maybe this is the start of a friendship, where heroes and villains can walk hand-in-hand in peace and harmony!"

Dex squinted his beady eyes at Ellie. Then he made a rotten pineapple face and marched away.

Ellie sighed. "Maybe not," she said.

"We have everything!" Hannah said. "Let's build that birdhouse. Go, Team Earth!"

CHAPTER 11

Team Earth

Ellie woke up bright and early Friday. It was Earth Day!

"Why isn't it called Stop a Bad Guy Day?" Ellie asked Hannah after morning announcements. "Pollution. Acid rain. Global warming. Those things are as bad as a yeti that cheats at checkers."

Hannah just smiled and shrugged.

The day got off to a green start. In reading, the class shared tree poems. Then they talked trash during science. They learned about garbage that could be recycled, and everyone became official garbologists.

Later in gym, Mrs. Walker took them on a nature walk. Then Mr. Cleveland told Earth Day jokes at lunch. He even dressed up as Earth! Unfortunately, Earth got tangled in the microphone cord.

"Have no fear! I'll save you!" Ellie cried.

She yanked the cord as hard as she could. Mr. Cleveland went spinning across the cafeteria. The principal landed safely on a stack of hamburger buns.

At last it was time for the Earth Day Showcase. In Room #128, all the teams set up their projects. They propped up posters and got displays ready.

Before long, Miss Little was welcoming visitors into the classroom. Moms and dads took in everything. There were lots of new ways to save the world!

"There's my superhero!" Dad greeted Ellie as he walked inside.

Ellie ran up and hugged him. "Where's Mom?" she asked, looking around.

"She isn't back yet," Dad replied. "But hopefully, she'll be here soon. I know she wouldn't want to miss your big day!"

Team Earth still had a few minutes before they were due to present. As Dad chatted with Hannah's mom, Hannah took her little sister, Cece, to the bathroom.

Ellie floated around to see everyone's work. Her first stop was Payton and Amanda's table. They stood there, holding their art caddy like game show hosts.

"Introducing Art, the Monster Caddy!" Payton announced. "By making Art, we kept this plastic bottle from ending up in a landfill. People throw away billions of bottles every year!"

"Art can hold your markers, pens, scissors, and more," Amanda added. "Step up and get one. We made enough for everybody!"

They weren't exaggerating. On the table, there was an army of Arts. It looked like an upcycled bottle invasion.

Suddenly, the lights went out. Across the room, Joshua and Owen glowed like neon mummies! Their clothes were wrapped in glow-in-the-dark yellow and blue shoelaces.

Miss Little switched the lights back on, and Ellie continued her Earth Day exploration. Across the room, Dex sat at his desk, flicking erasers into Miss Little's flowerpot. His shoebox was surprisingly quiet.

I better check on Dex's minions, Ellie thought.

It was never a good idea to leave evil alone for long. It was like a baby with a bowl of tomato soup. Disaster was bound to strike.

Ellie snuck through the crowd. She tiptoed up behind Dex and carefully peeked over his shoulder. Her mouth dropped to the floor. There, in the dark and dreary corners of the shoebox, were . . . plain old acorns!

"What?" Ellie whispered. She couldn't believe it. "No leaf-like claws? No thorny bark? No branches that could unleash a terrible tickle torture?"

There must've been some mistake! Where were the mastermind's oak tree minions?

Dex spun around. "Super-cootie alert! Super-cootie alert!" he chanted.

"Where's your project?" Ellie asked. "Aren't you growing something besides oak trees?"

"I only planted acorns." He picked up the shoebox and held it out. "What did you expect? Killer weeds?"

Close, Ellie thought. She motioned to the bottle of GroDream. "Why are you using special plant formula?"

"It'll make the trees grow fast," Dex replied. "If lots of trees are being cut down, I can replace them faster. Got it, Major Brainiac?" He went back to flicking erasers.

Ellie retreated happily. It was hard to believe, but Dex was helping the planet! He was using his evil genius for good. It was an Earth Day miracle!

The rest of the class had created some pretty impressive projects too. There was a bicycle that made clean energy. There was a water alarm that squirted mustard if you left the faucet running. There was also some kind of hook for picking up trash. It looked like something straight out of Mom and Dad's laboratory.

Finally, it was Ellie and Hannah's turn to show their project. "Are you ready, Team Earth?" asked Miss Little.

"Yep! I just have to get something." Hannah skipped off.

Ellie slowly headed for the door. She'd really been hoping Mom would arrive before her presentation. Suddenly, her super ears picked up a familiar voice.

"Mom!" Ellie shouted, spotting Mom walking up. "You made it!"

Mom leaned over and kissed Ellie's forehead. "Sorry I'm late! Sly Fox and his band of four-legged thieves were trying to steal some gadgets from the convention. But the Ultra Oopsie Daisy tripped them up, no problem!"

"C'mon, teammate!" Hannah exclaimed. She was wearing a brand-new Team Earth T-shirt. She handed Ellie a matching one. "Don't forget this. I made us new shirts since you-know-who ruined the first set."

"Thanks, partner!" Ellie slipped into the shirt. Then she hurried over to the habitat with Hannah. Miss Little directed their classmates and the rest of the visitors to follow along.

When the last person had gathered around, Ellie began the presentation. "Earth is a good habitat," she told the group. "It has everything we need, like food and water."

"It also has what we need to build a home," Hannah added. "That way, we have shelter."

"But Earth isn't just *our* habitat. Animals live here too," Ellie continued. "They need food, water, and shelter, just like we do. Sometimes, we take those things away from them. Sometimes, we don't share

Earth like we should. So our team made a habitat for them at school."

"There's food." Hannah pointed to the plants that circled the tree. "And water in the birdbath."

"The oak tree can give them shelter," Ellie said. "So can the brush pile. There's also a birdhouse that everyone helped make."

The birdhouse, which was Payton and Amanda's bottle, dangled from Joshua and Owen's neon shoelace. It also had their pencil for a perch. Inside were Dex's acorns that Ellie had crushed into bite-size birdie pieces.

"Kids can even use the habitat," Ellie finished. "They can read on a stump and walk on the path. Like Earth, it's a place we all can share."

The audience clapped, and Hannah showed their classmates around. "Way to team up for Earth!" Miss Little cheered.

"Super work, honey!" Mom said as Ellie skipped over to her parents. "This habitat will really help protect the planet."

"Maybe you could give B.R.A.I.N. some tips," Dad suggested.

As everyone explored the habitat, Ellie looked on proudly. With help, she had done her part in saving the world. Sure, it was her super duty. But it was a mighty responsibility, and even superheroes could use a hand.

GLOSSARY

amok (uh-MUHK) — a wild or uncontrolled manner

archenemy (AHRCH-EN-uh-mee) — someone's main enemy

brush (bruhsh) — small, broken branches and twigs

compost (KOM-pohst) — a decayed mixture of plants, such as leaves and grass, that is used to improve the soil in a garden

endangered (en-DEYN-jerd) — something, typically a plant or animal species, that is in danger of extinction

extinct (ik-STINGKT) — no longer existing

extraordinary (ek-STROR-duh-ner-ee) — very unusual or remarkable

habitat (HAB-i-tat) — the place or type of place where a plant or animal naturally or normally lives or grows

invention (in-VEN-shuhn) — an original device or process

laboratory (LAB-ruh-tawr-ee) — a room or building with special equipment for doing scientific experiments and tests

lair (LAIR) — a place where someone hides or where someone goes to be alone and to feel safe or comfortable

litter (LIT-er) — things that have been thrown away and that are lying on the ground in a public place

villain (VIL-uhn) — a wicked person, often an evil character in a play

TALK ABOUT ELLIE!

1. Ellie and Hannah are assigned a team project for Earth Week, but Ellie thinks she can do it all on her own. Do you think Ellie was being a good teammate? Why or why not? Make sure to use examples from the story to support your opinion.

2. Ellie's plan to create a copy of herself doesn't work out so well in the end. Talk about some of the things that went wrong, and then talk about how Ellie could have solved the problem differently.

3. With the help of their classmates, Ellie and Hannah are able to complete their schoolyard habitat. Using examples, talk about how they were able to use teamwork to get the job done. Then talk about a time teamwork made your life easier.

EXPRESS YOURSELF!

1. In order fix her copy's mistakes, Ellie finally asks Hannah for help. Write a paragraph about a time when you needed help to solve a problem. Make sure to talk about what the problem was and who helped you solve it.

2. Ellie fights super-villains, but there are other ways to save the world too. You can recycle, conserve water and electricity, and even plant a tree. Write a paragraph about something you can do to protect the planet.

3. For the Earth Day Showcase, Ellie and Hannah make a schoolyard habitat. Follow their lead and team up with a friend to create something that helps the environment. Don't forget to create a to-do list, just like Ellie and Hannah!

ABOUT THE AUTHOR

Gina Bellisario is an ordinary grown-up who can do many extraordinary things. She can make things disappear, such as a cheeseburger or a grass stain. She can create a masterpiece out of glitter glue and shoelaces. She can even thwart a messy room with her super cleaning power! Gina lives in Park Ridge, Illinois, not too far from Winkopolis, with her husband and their super kids.

ABOUT THE ILLUSTRATOR

Jessika von Innerebner loves creating — especially when it inspires and empowers others to make the world a better place. She landed her first illustration job at the age of seventeen and hasn't looked back since. Jess is an illustrator who loves humor and heart and has colored her way through projects with Disney.com, Nickelodeon, Fisher-Price, and Atomic Cartoons, to name a few. In her spare moments, Jess can be found long-boarding, yoga-ing, dancing, adventuring to distant lands, and laughing with friends. She currently lives in sunny Kelowna, Canada.

READ THE REST OF ELLIE ULTRA'S EXTRAORDINARY ADVENTURES!